THIS BOOK BELONGS TO:

SWIFT END TO THE LIFE OF THE SNIDER
A DEEP SLEEP! SNIDER
LOVES TO GLOAT ABOUT HIS BOAT IN THE MOAT
ZARD ONLY TO BE SAVED BY A ONE-LEGGED WIZARD
FOX, THIS IS WHY THE CHEEPHANT ROCK
OF THE PROPER WAY TO PRACTICE KUNG F
OES HAVE THE BEST OF LUCK
THA PRICK
A NOISE QUACK-QUACK CLUCK-CLUCK
A SCOWL A CEE
GO WITH A RHINOGATOR NAMED RINGO
NG ALL THE PROPAGANDA! GIRTLE
ELD IN THE CIRCUS OF VIETNAM LIGER
IN A SAVANNAH LIGER
G MY FRIEND HARRIET" SAID LARRIO
UITE FERTILE HE'S GOT TWENTY-THREE BABY GIRAFFE-TURTLE
IS BEING APPROACHED FROM THE REA

FOR:

ROYCE & RUBY

WHOSE BIRTHS ARE GREATLY ANTICIPATED

A SPECIAL THANKS TO:

MOM & DAD

FOR TEACHING ME TO READ AND INSPIRING THIS BOOK

BRYAN

FOR ALL YOUR LOVE AND SUPPORT

Brösenbooks

P.O. Box 1154
Laguna Beach, California 92652
www.brosenbooks.com

ISBN 978-0-9830359-0-9
Library of Congress Card Cataloging-in-Publication Data
CPSIA facility code: BP 305112

www.larriot.com

THE GREAT ADVENTURES OF
LARRIOT THE LIGER

WRITTEN & ILLUSTRATED BY

MEGAN MEYER

There is a Liger named Larriot in the Savannah.
He lives among lions in the village of Banana.
Young Larriot is only but two cub years old,
And already he's grown to a size mighty bold.
His dad and the cubmates have coats light and furry,
But Larriot is striped and is constantly dirty.

Because of his size and because of his fur,
Incessant pestering began to occur.
The cubmates were feisty and carelessly cruel.
They rolled him in mud and called him a fool.
"They make fun of my stripes and my size, don't you see?"
He cried to his father, "What's wrong with me?"

"My darling, don't be sad for you are not alone.
There are others out there with your color and tone."
"Where are they, where are they?" Larriot started to shout,
"I've never seen them," he said with much doubt.
The next day Larriot tried to hold his head high,
But the cubmates grew mean, and he started to cry.

"I've had it with Banana, I'm running away!"
So he ran and he ran, and he started to pray.
"Oh Maker, great Creator up in the sky,
If I am this ugly, please tell me why!"
He ran into the jungle with tears blurring his sight,
Until he realized he could be lost in the night.

He opened his eyes wide and looked all around.
He was alone in the jungle and couldn't be found.
A swamp, tall trees and no lions in sight!
What a perfect place! This might be just right!
As the sun began setting in this marshy place,
Larriot took notice of a curious race.

The little things moved through the grass rather fast,
And Larriot wanted to see them before they had passed.
He followed them trying to figure them out.
Half snail? Half spider? What's that all about?
"Those things are Sniders, you haven't seen them before?
You must not be from here; we've got hybrids galore!"

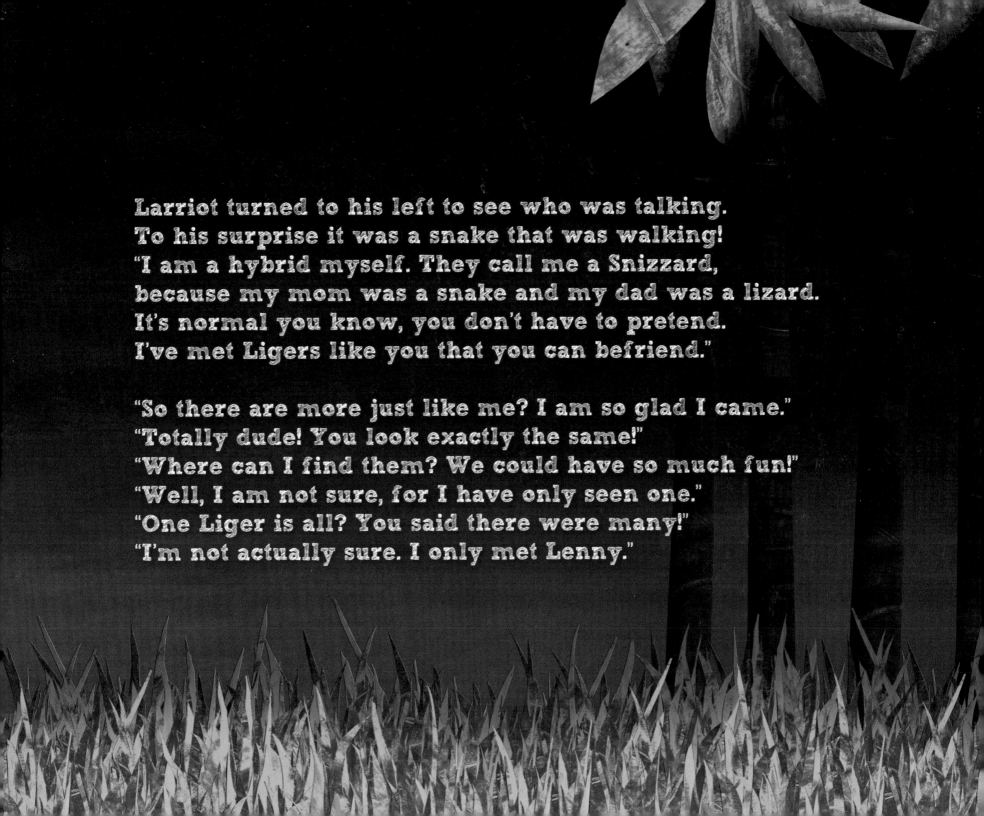

Larriot turned to his left to see who was talking.
To his surprise it was a snake that was walking!
"I am a hybrid myself. They call me a Snizzard,
because my mom was a snake and my dad was a lizard.
It's normal you know, you don't have to pretend.
I've met Ligers like you that you can befriend."

"So there are more just like me? I am so glad I came."
"Totally dude! You look exactly the same!"
"Where can I find them? We could have so much fun!"
"Well, I am not sure, for I have only seen one."
"One Liger is all? You said there were many!"
"I'm not actually sure. I only met Lenny."

So Larriot walked around looking to see
Someone who knew where the Ligers would be.
Soon out of the clearing a creature appeared.
It was tall. It was short. It was really quite weird.
"Hello I am Gerald. They call me a Girtle.
I'm a hybrid, of course, of a giraffe and a turtle."

The Girtle did not know where he should go,
So Larriot continued along rather slow.
He stopped every animal that did appear.
All kinds of hybrids and one strange looking deer.
None of them knew where the Ligers resided.
Everyone he approached appeared quite blindsided.

One after another, the creatures walked by.
Then along came a bird struggling to fly.
Larriot asked what he thought looked like a hen,
"Excuse me, have you heard of the Liger den?"
"Sorry, I cannot help you for I am a Chuck.
Ligers would love to get their paws on this chicken-duck."

"You see over there that Peamingo might know.
She's a bright young bird who goes to and fro."
The Peamingo said, "Yes, I know where they are.
I will take you there, but you should know it's quite far.
Where are you from? I haven't seen you before.
The Ligers don't come 'round these parts anymore."

"I live with the lions in a place far away.
I felt like a freak, so I left yesterday.
I came all this way looking to find
Someone like me, someone my kind."
"We're here, we've arrived" the Peamingo announced.
"I better get going, I don't want to be pounced!"

"Good luck on your journey. I hope you find what you need,"
Said the peacock-flamingo as she took off with speed.
Larriot saw a few Ligers rustling about.
But even more tigers were scattered throughout.
One Liger came over and asked him his name.
"I am Larriot," he said, feeling silly he came.

"I came all this way looking to see
If there were creatures like this, creatures like me.
But all I have found is dozens of creatures
Of all kinds of mixtures, with all kinds of features.
And you and the Ligers most similar to me
Are living with tigers in complete harmony."

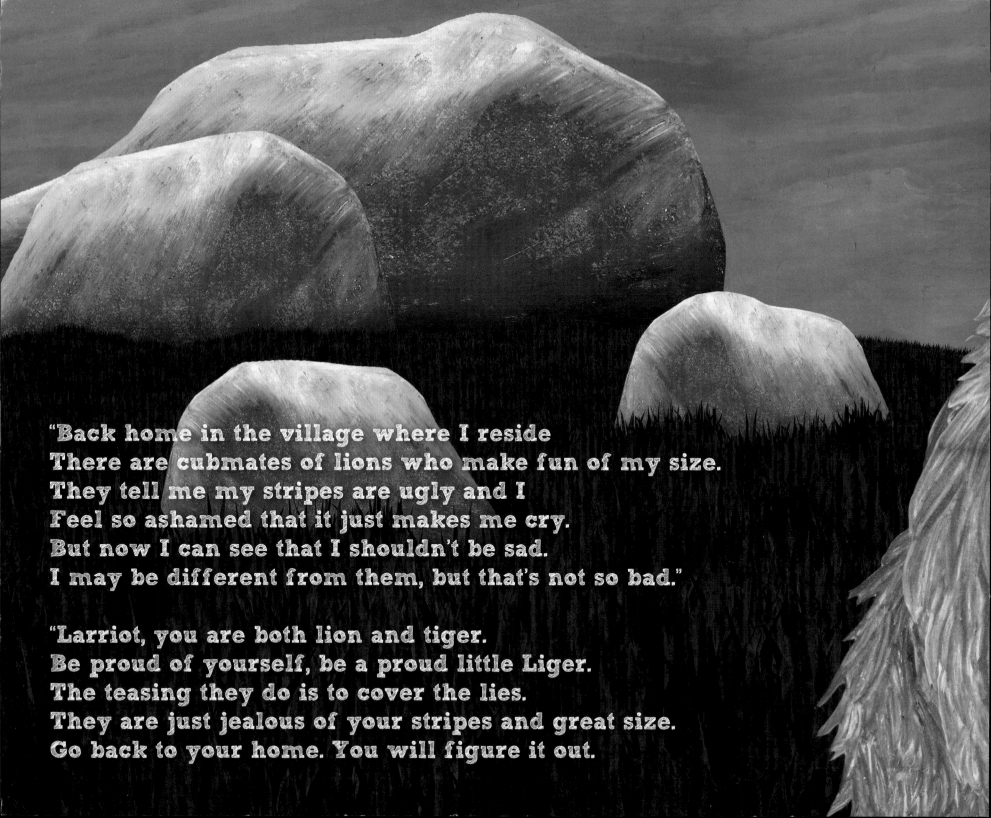

"Back home in the village where I reside
There are cubmates of lions who make fun of my size.
They tell me my stripes are ugly and I
Feel so ashamed that it just makes me cry.
But now I can see that I shouldn't be sad.
I may be different from them, but that's not so bad."

"Larriot, you are both lion and tiger.
Be proud of yourself, be a proud little Liger.
The teasing they do is to cover the lies.
They are just jealous of your stripes and great size.
Go back to your home. You will figure it out.

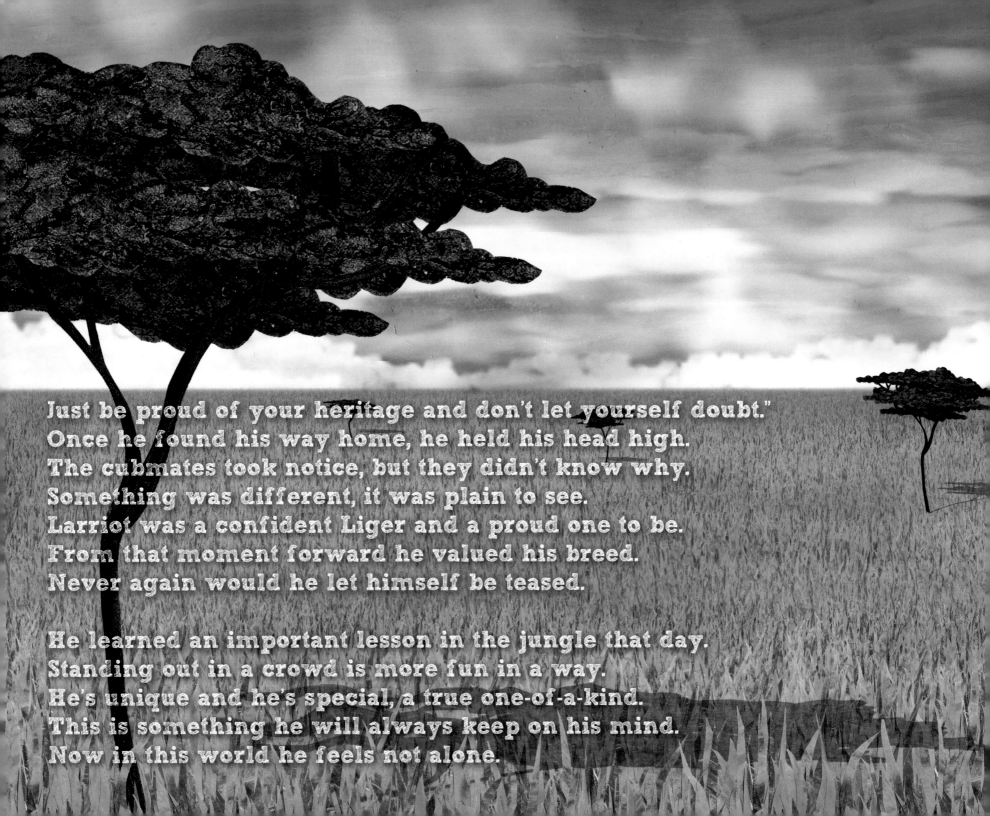

Just be proud of your heritage and don't let yourself doubt."
Once he found his way home, he held his head high.
The cubmates took notice, but they didn't know why.
Something was different, it was plain to see.
Larriot was a confident Liger and a proud one to be.
From that moment forward he valued his breed.
Never again would he let himself be teased.

He learned an important lesson in the jungle that day.
Standing out in a crowd is more fun in a way.
He's unique and he's special, a true one-of-a-kind.
This is something he will always keep on his mind.
Now in this world he feels not alone.

ABOUT THE AUTHOR

Megan Meyer lives in California with her husband, Bryan. She loves creating new things, using her imagination, traveling, swimming and spending time with those she loves. Her mother, a school teacher, gave her the idea for this book.

Megan used a unique combination of oil pastels and computer graphics to illustrate it. This is her first book, but hopefully not her last.

DID YOU KNOW LIGERS REALLY EXIST?

Just like in the book, Ligers are a combination of a male lion and a female tigress. They tend to be very large, so large that they are called the biggest cat in the world. They have characteristics of both tigers and lions – usually striped like tigers, but lighter in color like lions. They only exist in captivity because in the wild lions and tigers usually do not live close enough to accidentally breed. A Tigon is the opposite of a Liger, with a tiger for a father and a lioness for a mother. They are less common than Ligers because Ligers tend to live much longer.

Not every animal Larriot encountered in the jungle can actually exist, but those of a similar species like lions and tigers can actually breed! There are many other known hybrid animals out there too!

Check out this list:

Beefalo or Zubron = Cow + Bison
Blynx = Bobcat + Lynx
Cama = Camel + Llama
Coydog or Dogote = Dog + Coyote
Coywolf = Coyote + Wolf
Dzo = Yak + Cow
Geep = Goat + Sheep
Habbit = Hare + Rabbit
Huarizo = Llma + Alpaca
Jaglion or Liguar = Jaguar + Lion
Leopon or Lipard = Leopard + Lion
Mule or Hinny = Donkey + Horse
Liger or Tiglon = Tiger + Lion
Pumapard = Puma + Leopard
Prizzly Bear or Grolar Bear = Polar Bear + Grizzly Bear
Tiguar or Jagger = Tiger + Jaguar
Wholphin = Killer Whale + Dolphin
Wolfdog =Wolf + Dog
Yakalo = Yak + Bison
Zeedonk or Zonkey = Zebra + Donkey
Zorse = Zebra + Horse
Zony = Zebra + Pony